W9-BPM-827

Discard

Discard

A Pony For Jeremiah

by Robert H. Miller
illustrated by Nneka Bennett

Silver Burdett Press
Parsippany, New Jersey

Published by Silver Burdett Press

A Division of Simon & Schuster

299 Jefferson Road

Parsippany, NJ 07054

Designed by Studio Goodwin Sturges

Printed in the United States of America

ISBN 0-382-39459-3 (LSB) 1 2 3 4 5 6 7 8 9 10

ISBN 0-382-39460-7 (PBK) 1 2 3 4 5 6 7 8 9 10

Library of Congress Cataloging-in-Publication Data

Miller, Robert H. (Robert Henry). 1944-

A Pony for Jeremiah/by Robert H. Miller: illustrated by Nneka Bennett.

p. cm.

Summary: After running away from the Mississippi plantation where they had been slaves,
nine-year-old Jeremiah Johnson and his family begin a new life in Nebraska, where
Jeremiah meets a Cheyenne boy who becomes a good friend.

[1. Afro-Americans—Fiction. 2.Fugitive slaves—Fiction. 3.Frontier and pioneer life—
Nebraska—Fiction. 4. Nebraska—Fiction] I. Bennett, Nneka, ill. II. Title.

Pz7.M633335Po 1997   95-3473

[Fic]-dc 20   CIP   AC

This book is dedicated to my uncles, Earl and Alvin Batiste, my mother, Margaret M. Boyd, and to the memory of my grandmother, Shelly Katherine Batiste.

R. H. M.

For my brothers.

N.B.

Introduction

When slavery existed in America, African Americans paid a heavy price. They had to give up their freedom. An African American had no rights in the South, and it was a constant struggle to keep a family together. Many times this was impossible.

Young Jeremiah, after watching his father get brutally branded by Master Slocomb, was able to escape with his family from the plantation in Mississippi to a new land in Nebraska. To Jeremiah, Nebraska was far away from the South, and all those terrible memories of slavery. In this new land, young Jeremiah learns his first lesson about the true meaning of freedom and responsibility.

« 1 »

Freedom Bound

After many nights on the run, Jeremiah, his father Henry, and his mother Shelly arrived in Missouri. They had to be extra careful. Missouri was a slave state and if they were caught all of them would have been sold right back into slavery. Henry had heard stories about the Underground Railroad from other slaves. This was a secret route to freedom that slave catchers could never find. Whites who opposed slavery and freed blacks operated the stations, hiding runaway slaves and helping them to reach up north and freedom. Unfortunately, he didn't know the whereabouts of any Underground Railroad stations and had to rely on his wits to protect his family.

Their raft had been badly damaged by the rough current of the Mississippi River, so they abandoned it and walked. Hiding by day, nightfall was always a welcomed visitor because that was the only time travel was possible. But this night would be unlike any other.

Earlier that day, Henry had spotted a smokehouse about a mile away from where they were hiding. "I'll be back shortly. That smokehouse should have something in it we can eat besides these wild berries, then we can move on," he said.

"Be careful," said Jeremiah's mother. The two of them had an unspoken understanding. If he didn't return by morning, she and Jeremiah were to continue without him. Slipping through the tall grass, Jeremiah's father headed for the smokehouse.

❖   ❖   ❖

With moonlight shining through the smokehouse window, Henry could see a big ham hanging from the ceiling. Carefully he placed his hands on both sides of the window and pushed. Halfway up it stuck. He pushed harder and the window make a loud noise as it opened wide.

He climbed through the window. It was dark inside the smokehouse. He didn't see an empty pail and his foot accidentally knocked it over. The handle made a loud clanging sound as the

pail rolled across the wooden floor. With his knife, he cut the rope holding the ham. Catching it in his arms, he quickly checked around to see if there was anything else he needed. Pleased with what he had, Jeremiah's father was about to climb out of the window when, suddenly, the smokehouse door flew open.

"Hold it, right there!" said a voice in an accent Henry had never heard before.

A beam of bright light flooded the dimly lit area just as quickly as the voice stopped Henry dead in his tracks. "Turn around slowly and drop the sack," the voice ordered. Henry did exactly as he was told, sensing that his "runaway" days were over.

When he turned around, he came face-to-face with what he thought was the end of the road, a white man holding a shotgun in one hand and a lantern in the other. Both men stared at each other for a moment without speaking a word.

"That's a mighty big ham for one man. Are there more of you?" the man asked.

Henry wasn't sure what to say. This white man's accent sounded so strange to him.

"There's nobody else but me," Henry finally answered.

"You must be mighty hungry to eat all that.

Drop the sack and turn around."

"If you're going' to kill me . . . shoot me face-to-face," said Henry.

"If I was going to shoot you, you'd be dead right now. I said turn around."

Henry dropped the sack and turned around.

"Take off your shirt," the man ordered.

Facing the window, Henry pulled the torn shirt over his head. From the reflection in the window, he saw the white man shake his head in disgust. "What animal did this to you?" he asked.

"Master Slocomb," replied Henry.

"Put your shirt back on and turn around," said the white man.

Jeremiah's father was really confused but he did as he was told.

Who was this white man, and why did he talk funny? he thought.

"I'm Hans. I'm German," he said as he stretched forth his hand.

"Pleased to meet you, sir," said Henry half-smiling while shaking Hans's hand.

"I'm sorry I had to put you through that, but the only way I could tell if you weren't a spy for the slave catchers was to look at your back. Your wounds look pretty new."

"We escaped from the Slocomb plantation and the slave catchers. I sure ain't no spy," said

Henry to Hans.

"It's not right what some of us whites do to your people. My wife and me, after we got here, we decided to help in the best way we could. I'll get you to freedom on the Underground Railroad. Time is short, so listen. You must get to the Underground Railroad station by tomorrow before sundown. Some other people will guide you the rest of the way. When you get to Kansas, you'll be all right."

"Me and my family are beholding to you," said Henry.

"I knew there was more of you out there, that's a pretty big ham for one man. Take it and feed your family. Here, take this too," said Hans, reaching into his pocket. "It's a little something to tide you over."

Jeremiah's father looked at the five gold coins, then at Hans.

"May God have mercy on you and bless you. I'm plenty grateful."

"You better get a move on, it'll be light soon. Godspeed," said Hans.

This time Henry left the smokehouse through the front door. Once he had felt all white men were evil, but what happened tonight made him realize that you can't judge all the apples in a barrel by the few that are rotten. His life and perhaps the lives of his family might depend on a white man, with a funny accent, he'd never met before but one he'd always remember.

❖　　❖　　❖

Kansas was a big, bustling territory compared to Mississippi.

"Look, over there!" pointed Jeremiah. Everywhere he turned he saw black men and women dressed like white folks. In all his years on the plantation, the only women he ever saw riding in one-horse carriages and wearing long dresses had been white.

Black men were talking to white men face-to-face. That wasn't allowed in Mississippi. Jeremiah and his family couldn't believe their eyes, Kansas was truly a different place. If this is what freedom meant, then they were anxious to give it a try.

"I'm supposed to look up a man named Stevenson," said Henry to his wife, Shelly.

"Where are you going to find Mr. Stevenson?" she asked.

"He owns a store around here somewhere."

It was against the law to teach slaves to read or write, so Henry had to always listen carefully to what was being said. He remembered Hans had told him to look up Mr. Stevenson when he got to Kansas. After stopping a few people for directions, they found themselves standing in front of a building that read, "Stevenson's General Store."

"I guess this is the place," said Henry. When they entered the store, Jeremiah's mouth dropped wide open. Everywhere he looked he saw food, clothes, and materials to make clothes, and many more things. Even his mother spun around in a circle looking at all the pots and pans, shoes, and of course all these pretty dresses hanging on the racks.

"May I help you?" said a tall man, coming in from the side door.

They all turned in the direction of a black man whose voice sounded white to them.

"Yes, sir, I'm looking for a Mister Stevenson," said Jeremiah's father.

"You're speaking to him. I'm Stevenson. How may I help you?"

"Hans said to look you up when we got here."

"If Hans sent you, I know why you're here. Welcome to Kansas. You all must be hungry, and I'm sure you want to wash up. My home is just outside of town. Give me a minute to unload these supplies and I'll take you there," he said.

"I'll give you a hand," said Henry.

Another young black man about eighteen

years old entered loaded down with more packages. "That's my son Rodney. He'll watch the store," said Mr. Stevenson.

While Jeremiah's father helped unload the wagon, Jeremiah played with some spinning tops and wooden horses on the shelves. His mother handled the soft silk material and dreamed of the day she'd wear a dress made from such beautiful fabric.

That evening at dinner, Jeremiah's family had a chance to meet Mrs. Stevenson. They had all taken baths and Mrs. Stevenson had given them clean clothes to wear. Jeremiah had a difficult time feeding himself, his eyes constantly looking around the big dinning room. Beautiful paintings, furniture, and curtains all competed for Jeremiah's attention.

"You know there's a rumor going around. Looks like the South wants to fight rather than give up its slaves," said Mr. Stevenson.

"We been busy trying to get out of the South. There's been no time for no rumors," said Henry.

"Southerners have been trying to push slavery into Kansas and as far west as they can. We've had to fight every step of the way. Good whites and freed black people had to take up arms many times against them. Southerners kidnap black men, women, and children, take them back across the border to Missouri, and sell them into slavery again."

When Jeremiah's mother heard this, chills raced through her body. "We heard Kansas was a free place. I thought our running was over," she sighed.

"Until this ugly institution of slavery is abolished, no black person is safe," said Mrs. Stevenson.

"I know you must feel disappointed to come this far and not be free, but farther west of here, you can make a new start," said Mr. Stevenson.

"Where's that?" interrupted Jeremiah.

"Nebraska!" responded Mr. Stevenson.

"I never heard of Ne-bras-ka," said Jeremiah's mother.

"You're no more than a week's ride with a horse and wagon. That should put you far west in that territory," said Mr. Stevenson.

"We be free there?" asked Jeremiah.

"You'll have a good start, son," said Mr. Stevenson.

"We'll work from sunup to sundown to buy a horse and wagon."

"Who do I see to get started?" asked Henry.

"You're looking at him, and I'd consider it an honor if you'd allow me to give you and your family a grubstake for your first home."

"Thank you, Mr. Stevenson, God bless you and your family," said Jeremiah's father.

Now that's settled, I'd like to show you my library."

"What's a library?" asked Jeremiah.

"Follow me," said Mr. Stevenson, getting up from the table. He was proud of his library and the books he'd collected from all over the world. Standing on a small ladder, he picked out a book and handed it to Jeremiah.

"One day you'll be able to read this. It's *The Three Musketeers* by Alexander Dumas. His father was the son of a Frenchman and an African woman," said Mr. Stevenson.

Jeremiah held the book close to his chest. He had always wondered what all those lines in books meant, now he had his very own.

"Tomorrow morning, I'll start teaching all of you how to read," said Mrs. Stevenson.

Jeremiah and his family stayed with the Stevensons for several weeks. More trouble with the South was building as they brought reinforcements into Kansas promoting slavery.

"You all better be heading out. It's going to get pretty rough around here real soon," warned Mr. Stevenson.

"If a war breaks out against slavery, count me in," said Jeremiah's father.

"I'll remember that, but for now, take your family to Nebraska. Remember, Jeremiah, a man's never free if he can't read or write," said Mr. Stevenson.

Jeremiah sat in the wagon that was loaded down with supplies for building a home, clothes, food, and everything they needed to start a new life. The last words he heard from Mr. Stevenson stuck in his mind. His father snapped the reins and the team of horses pulled out of Kansas—destination Nebraska.

« 2 »

A Pony for Jeremiah

"Jeremiah, Jeremiah, you all right son?" asked his mother. Jeremiah's thoughts were so far away, he hadn't heard her footsteps.

"Jeremiah, I said, are you all right?"

"I'm sorry Mama . . . I was just thinking about the plantation, you and Papa, and how we got here."

Shelly put her arm around him as she sat down on the porch. The sun was setting, casting a brilliant red and orange glow in the Nebraska sky. "Take a deep breath . . . you got God's free air whistling through your body," she said.

Jeremiah took a deep breath and held it, then let it go.

"Feels good, Mama!" he said, smiling.

"Now what made you think about that old plantation? It's been over two years now since we left there."

"Sometimes, Mama, I feel like it's all a dream, and I'm going to wake up and be picking cotton for Master Slocomb."

"You just put them thoughts out of your mind. Getting our freedom wasn't easy, but now that we got it, we're not looking back. A war is going on right now to free our people. We'll never be slaves again," she said.

Jeremiah smiled at his mother as he rested his head on her soft shoulder. She was right, their family had come a long way from slavery to freedom and survived. He felt a warm feeling of comfort rush through his bones. The past was finally buried and gone, now it was time to move on to more important things.

"Mama, I been thinking about some other things besides how we got here. I can ride real good and I know how to take care of horses. Do you think papa will take me out to catch my own pony?"

"Why don't you ask him when he gets back? Can you take care of a pony and keep up with your chores around here?" Jeremiah's mother asked.

Jeremiah thought about that. He knew harvest time for their wheat and vegetables was just around the corner. They would be working real hard to get ready for the winter. He wasn't sure his father would have time to help him go look for a wild pony. "Papa might be too tired when he gets back with all these supplies, and we got work to do around here. Maybe this is not the best time to ask him." Jeremiah sighed.

"Jeremiah, you ought to be ashamed of yourself. When did you start getting shy about asking for something? If you want that pony bad enough, then you'll ask your papa as soon as he gets back, you hear?" scolded his mother.

"Yes, ma'am."

❖   ❖   ❖

The two of them sat on the porch of their cabin and watched the sun slowly disappear, leaving in its place the biggest and prettiest full moon they had ever seen.

Jeremiah was awakened early the next morning by his father's voice and June Bug's whinny as she pulled that squeaky old wagon. He jumped out of his bed like a baby jackrabbit, put on his clothes, and ran outside to help.

The wagon was loaded down with supplies and clothes they needed for the winter. A big grin splashed across Jeremiah's face when he saw the keg of molasses—that meant flapjacks on Sunday morning.

"Give me a hand," said his father. Jeremiah was happy to see his father, and he enjoyed helping him unload the wagon.

"When you finish, I got some hot biscuits and eggs, bacon, and grits waiting for you!" shouted Jeremiah's mother from the kitchen.

After breakfast, Henry told them about his trip into town and some of the Indians he met. When he had finished, Jeremiah's mother looked at her son and nodded her head. Jeremiah knew what that nod meant—she felt the time was right to ask his father about a pony.

"Papa . . . " said Jeremiah hesitantly.

"What, son?"

"Well, I been thinking . . . I can take care of horses real good, and you taught me to ride when I was a baby. I'd like to have my own pony. I'll work real hard and keep up with all my chores and train him myself," said an excited Jeremiah.

His father listened to his son and thought to himself how fast Jeremiah had grown up since they escaped the plantation. He knew his son was ready for the challenge.

"You're right, you ought to have your own pony. I knew something was cooking in that head of yours to ask me. We'll go out to Pine Ridge first thing in the morning, I hear mustangs run wild out there," he said.

That night Jeremiah could hardly sleep. From the time his family first entered Nebraska and he saw a herd of wild horses galloping across the plains, he had promised himself that one day he'd catch his own. As he tossed and turned in bed, visions of beautiful mustangs raced through his head. Tomorrow couldn't come quick enough.

❖   ❖   ❖

The next morning, Jeremiah and his father packed a lunch and rode out to Pine Ridge. It was a clear day; clouds hung in the sky like big fluffy balls of cotton. A cool breeze swept the plains. Even though the morning was perfect, they didn't find one mustang.

"Let's head over to Willow Springs, we may have better luck," said Jeremiah's father.

When they arrived at Willow Springs, their luck did indeed change. A herd of ten wild mustangs were all taking a leisurely drink of water.

"Look, Papa, look!" said Jeremiah, pointing.

"Shhhhh, you'll spook them. I see what you're looking at," whispered his father. Henry licked his finger, then held it up in the air. Jeremiah had spotted a pale brown mustang pony that had strayed away from its mother. "We better go 'round this way. If they get our scent, they'll take off like a bunch of wild geese."

When they got within a hundred feet of the herd, Jeremiah dismounted. "You remember what I taught you?" his father asked.

"Yes, sir," said Jeremiah, reaching for his rope. Quietly, he ran behind a clump of trees and quickly ducked out of sight. His father was a safe distance away but ready if his son needed help. The pony came a little closer to the trees. Suddenly Jeremiah jumped up. "Yehaaa!" he screamed, waving his hands. Mustangs took off in every direction. The wild colt panicked and ran past the trees. Swinging his rope high in the air, Jeremiah threw it and lassoed the pony around the neck. "Whoa, Whoa," shouted Jeremiah, trying to control the wild colt and keep his balance.

Rearing up on his hind legs and whinnying, the pony twisted his neck struggling to get free. When he came down on all fours, he took off. The sudden move surprised Jeremiah and he lost his footing. Holding onto the rope as if his life depended on it, Jeremiah was dragged across the prairie.

Like a bolt of lightning shot from the sky, Henry took off after Jeremiah. As Henry's horse

gained on them, he lassoed the wild colt, bringing it to an immediate stop.

"You all right?" his father asked, breathing heavily.

"I think so," said Jeremiah, dazed and covered with dust from head to toe.

"Why didn't you let go? You could've gotten hurt real bad."

"I couldn't, Papa. I caught him, he's mine," said a very tired but proud Jeremiah.

His father smiled when he heard that. Jeremiah was just as determined as he was. "One thing's for sure, you got yourself one fine-looking pony. Now let's go home," his father said.

But Jeremiah could feel someone watching them from a distance.

"Look, Papa," he said pointing to a band of Cheyenne.

"I see them, just keep riding. They look friendly."

As the Indians came closer, Jeremiah noticed that one of the riders was about his age, was wearing a blue feather in his headband. Then an Indian that looked about as old as Henry, pulled up his horse, smiled, and raised his right hand. Henry did the same thing. Both men brought their horses to a halt. The other Indians slowly circled Jeremiah and his father, watching them closer than a mother wolf over her baby cubs.

"I am Chief Running Fox. We are Cheyenne. We welcome you to our land," said the chief.

Jeremiah's father was a bit surprised when the chief spoke English. He'd heard stories that the Cheyenne were a suspicious and dangerous people, but so far it seemed the Cheyenne were only curious.

"I'm Henry Johnson . . . this is my son, Jeremiah. He just caught his first wild pony."

"Yes, it is a good-looking pony. My son, Blue Feather, has searched for one like that for many moons," said the chief, pointing to his son.

Blue Feather pulled his horse near Jeremiah's captured pony. You could tell by the way he petted the animal's neck that he wanted it for himself.

"He's mine," said Jeremiah sternly to Blue Feather.

Blue Feather looked Jeremiah in the eyes, then trotted his horse around to join the others.

"Thank you for your welcome, Running Fox," said Jeremiah's father as he extended his hand. Running Fox shook it and immediately raised his left hand. He and his men rode off as quickly as they arrived.

The next day, Jeremiah was eager to get his chores out of the way. Yesterday's experience with the Cheyenne lingered in his mind. He wondered if he'd ever see Blue Feather again. One thing for sure, he didn't like the way he looked at Jeremiah's colt. Now that he had a pony, he wanted the colt to like him right away. So with a handful of sugar lumps and hay, Jeremiah walked into the corral.

"Come on, boy, come to me," whispered Jeremiah. He had watched his father do this many times and it always worked. Speaking in a low voice when approaching a wild horse, while offering it something to eat, usually won the horse over to your side. But this colt stood his ground and started pawing into the dirt. As Jeremiah got closer, the colt charged right at him. Quicker than the blink of an eye, Jeremiah dropped everything and leaped onto the corral fence. He barely got out of the way of the colt's hoofs as he galloped past.

"He's tough. You got your work cut out for you," said Henry.

Jeremiah was just like his father. He wasn't one to give up so easily. Picking the sugar lumps off the ground, he watched the colt prance around the corral like he'd just won a blue ribbon.

"Come here, boy . . . come to me," insisted Jeremiah, holding the sugar lumps in his outstretched hand.

The colt continued to prance around, ignoring him. Standing in the middle of the corral, Jeremiah waited. The wild colt slowed his trot, reared up on his hind legs, and whinnied, daring Jeremiah to come near him. Waiting patiently, Jeremiah began to whistle, very softly. This was a trick he'd seen a slave do on the plantation to calm a wild dog. It seemed to be working, the colt began to slowly circle around him, and with every turn, he got closer and closer. When the colt was close enough, Jeremiah grabbed the colt's mane and hurled himself onto its back.

"That a boy, I got you now!" yelled Jeremiah, trying to stay on the pony's back. He gave it all he had, but the colt threw him off. Jeremiah hit the ground, bouncing like a rock skipping across a pond.

« 3 »

When Freedom Calls

"Jeremiah, we got plenty of work to do. We got to get that hay in the barn and smoke the meat for the winter," said Henry as his eyes searched the skies. "Old man winter will be here in a minute," he continued.

Jeremiah was preoccupied. Sitting on the corral fence, he watched his new pony trot around. It had been four weeks and all Jeremiah was able to do was feed the wild colt and pet his nose. Whenever he whistled, the colt would come over to him, but the moment Jeremiah would try to climb on his back, that colt would take off in the opposite direction.

"Jeremiah, did you hear me?" shouted his father.

Jeremiah knew that tone of voice. He jumped off the fence, ran over to the barn, and started helping his father bail the hay.

◈　　◈　　◈

At the dinner table that evening, Jeremiah's mother noticed her son wasn't his usual self. She had prepared his favorite meal: fried chicken, mashed potatoes, green beans, and corn bread. But Jeremiah just picked at the food on his plate with his fork, not eating much of anything.

"Jeremiah . . . are you feeling all right, son?" asked his mother.

"Yes, ma'am," he said.

"Well, you won't be if you don't eat something. Is it that pony?" she asked.

Jeremiah knew he had to give a reason for his behavior. He knew he'd been acting strangely. "I can't figure it out. The pony won't let me ride him no matter what I do. I think he hates me," said a sad Jeremiah.

"Horses don't hate people, people do," snapped his father. "You caught a smart pony, son. My bet is he was born to be a leader. I've never seen a pony like him, so headstrong. I'm surprised he lets you feed him," he continued

"He comes to me when I whistle, but he won't let me on his back. I don't know what to do," said Jeremiah.

"I learned something from a slave named

George many years ago. I was about your age. Nobody knew animals like George. He could talk a horse or any animal into doing anything he wanted. He told me one day that animals are like some people . . . the harder you try to break their spirit, the harder it is. Your pony won't let you ride him, until he's good and ready," said Jeremiah's father.

Jeremiah sat on the front porch after dinner, thinking about what his father said. His thoughts were interrupted occasionally by a distant wail of a coyote. What if he never wants me to ride him? thought Jeremiah. He continued to think about how his father came back to get him and his mother when they had made their escape from slavery. Getting branded by Master Slocomb didn't break his father's spirit.

Maybe the colt wants his freedom . . . maybe nobody will ever ride him, Jeremiah thought fearfully.

The Nebraska winds teased the loose hay in the corral like a kitten playing with a ball of yarn, swirling it up into the air and gently bringing it back to earth. Jeremiah was up earlier than usual this morning. He didn't sleep well last night, and today he had to make big decision.

Climbing up on the fence, he watched the wild colt prance around the corral, waiting for his breakfast.

"I'm going to ride you one day, then you'll be mine," said Jeremiah.

The colt stopped and looked in his direction as if he heard every word, shook his mane, and kept right on trotting. Out of nowhere, Jeremiah heard a loud whinny. On a hill not far from the barn, he saw a beautiful pale yellow horse rearing up on its hind legs and whinnying. It was the same horse he'd seen weeks ago grazing near the colt. Jeremiah sensed it had to be the colt's mother. The colt whinnied back and tried to climb the fence.

"It's your mother, she came back for you," Jeremiah told the colt.

Jeremiah had to make a decision and it wasn't easy. He'd taken a strong liking to that colt and felt somehow the colt also like him. Walking over to the corral gate, he unlocked it.

"Go on, boy!" shouted a saddened Jeremiah.

The colt galloped out of the corral, racing to meet his mother. Standing by the corral gate, Jeremiah watched them as they disappeared over the hill like puffs of smoke. Staring off into the distance, he didn't notice his father walking up behind him.

"That took some doing, son. I know it wasn't easy for you. It hurts to let go of something you want so bad, but if it's meant for you to have it, can't nothing stop you from getting it," said his father.

"He'll remember me, Papa. I know he will," said Jeremiah.

"One thing for sure, he's not the only horse in Nebraska territory. We'll get you another one," his father replied.

"He was special, Papa . . . there is no other pony like him."

His father put his arm around his son's shoulders as they walked back to the barn. Work would take the place of Jeremiah's sorrow. There was a lot of that to do before those wintry winds started blowing across the Nebraska plains.

« 4 »

A Stranger Comes to Call

Jeremiah and his family didn't get many visitors, but one evening at dinnertime a stranger came riding by. When his mother opened the door to greet the visitor, Jeremiah saw a neatly dressed black man carrying a leather bag covered with shiny brass buckles. "Come in and rest yourself," smiled Jeremiah's mother.

"Thank you, ma'am. My name is Monroe, William Monroe," said the tall stranger.

"You new in these parts?" asked Henry, taking the man's hat and coat.

"Not exactly, I've been in this area before, that's how I knew how to find you. In fact, a friend of yours in Kansas, Mr. Stevenson, said you'd probably settled out here." Mr. Monroe said.

"We know Mr. Stevenson well. How is he and

his family?" asked Shelly.

"They're doing just fine, but some things have changed since you all last saw each other. A war over slavery has broken out between the North and the South. I'm recruiting every able-bodied black man to join on the side of the North, so we can stomp out slavery everywhere. If the South wins this fight, they'll make every state in the Union a slave state and it'll spread to the territories like Nebraska. We're meeting in Kansas to sign up as many black recruits as possible, and I'm here to ask you to join us," he said to Henry.

Quiet fell over the house. Jeremiah sat at the dinner table peeking over the top of his book. While he listened, his eyes moved from the face of his mother to that of his father, then back to Mr. Monroe.

"You want my husband to go fight in this war?" asked Shelly.

"Ma'am, I'm just here to tell your husband what the rest of us are doing. If he chooses not to go, nobody is going to judge him. I know you want to talk about it among yourselves. I'll leave these papers with you, in case you decide to join," he said, handing them to Henry. "I want to thank you for your time, but I must be on my way, I've got a couple of other places to go to

before dark," he said, standing.

Jeremiah's mother got his hat and coat and handed them to him.

"You want some sweet cakes to take with you?" she asked.

"That'd be mighty kind of you, ma'am." said the stranger.

As she got the sweet cakes, Jeremiah couldn't help but notice the stranger was taller than his father and strong looking. He thought, with black men like him fighting for the freedom of the slaves, the North would surely win.

"Thank you, ma'am," he said to Jeremiah's mother as she handed him a bag of sweet cakes.

"You have a safe journey," said Henry, standing in the doorway.

When the hoofbeats of Mr. Monroe's horse had faded, Henry looked at the papers he held in his hand. He could read now that he had some schooling. The words that rang in his heart, were written by a former slave named Frederick Douglass. He'd heard that name many times during his long talks with Mr. Stevenson. On the paper calling for black volunteers, he had written the words: " . . . like brave men, rise and unlock for ourselves the golden gates of a glorious future."

"You going to join the army, Papa?" asked a

curious Jeremiah.

"I'm thinking about it," replied his father.

"Do you have to?" asked his wife.

Henry walked over to the dinner table and laid the papers down.

Looking at his son, then his wife, he said, "Shelly, I need to talk to you and Jeremiah."

Shelly knew that look in her husband's eyes when his mind was made up. It was the same look she saw that night they escaped the plantation. He was going to join the Union Army no matter what she had to say.

"Son, I always taught you never to take anything you didn't work for. If a man doesn't work for his own freedom, then it's not really his. This President Lincoln, he's giving us, freed slaves and runaways alike, a chance to fight and maybe die for what God gave every man naturally. I can't stand back and watch, while other black men fight for what's theirs. If freedom is worth having, then it's worth dying for, I'm joining the Union Army."

He held both of their hands, and with bowed heads, they prayed.

Henry left two days later, heading for Kansas, to fight in the Union Army.

« 5 »

Jeremiah Makes a New Friend

A year had come and gone since Henry had headed off to war. Jeremiah read the one letter his father sent so often he had it memorized. Jeremiah wondered how many rebels his father had killed. Was he a prisoner or even alive? His mind also skipped to the wild colt he'd captured a year ago. By now, the colt would be big and strong and could probably outrun any horse in Nebraska, thought Jeremiah.

These images ran through his mind like a buffalo stampede. He sat on the bank of the small stream, fishing. Unaware of the water splashing just up the stream a bit, Jeremiah didn't hear another young fisherman coming his way.

"Ahh! Ahh!" screamed Blue Feather as he speared a fish in the water.

Jeremiah snapped out of his daydream and turned in the direction of the noise.

"Ahh! Ahha!" shouted Blue Feather again.

"Stop, you'll scare away the fish!" shouted Jeremiah.

Blue Feather was a little surprised to see Jeremiah with his pole and line in the stream. "You will go hungry for many moons trying to fish your way." Blue Feather smiled.

Jeremiah noticed the basket Blue Feather had hanging on his shoulder. It was full of fish, while Jeremiah had caught only one.

"If you would stop yelling, I could catch something," snapped Jeremiah.

At first, Jeremiah couldn't place where he'd seen the boy, but then he remembered the blue feather. "I remember you, your people stopped me and my pa last year, you kept looking at my new pony," said Jeremiah.

"Do you still have him?" asked Blue Feather.

Jeremiah had a feeling Blue Feather already knew the answer.

"I can't rightly say where he is now, but wherever he is, he's still mine," said Jeremiah.

"Hmmm, a good horse will always remember his master. How long you been here fishing?" asked Blue Feather, looking at Jeremiah's one lonely fish.

"I just started when you came around the bend scaring the fish."

"Your fish looks too dried up to be caught so soon. How would you like to catch fish my way?" asked Blue Feather.

Seeing as though he hardly had any fish, Jeremiah would have tried anything rather than go home with only one fish. "I'd like that a lot." Jeremiah smiled.

"Watch me, do as I do," said Blue Feather. Blue Feather walked around the stream looking intently at the water. Then, like a rattlesnake, he struck, spearing another fish.

"How'd you do that?" asked Jeremiah.

"Here, take my spear. Watch for a shadow moving under the water. That's a fish. Then spear it!" instructed Blue Feather.

Jeremiah took the spear carefully walking in the water up to his waist, he searched for a shadow. To his amazement, he saw something moving in the water. "Ahaa!" screamed Jeremiah, striking the spear at the shadow in the water.

When he pulled the spear out of the water, he and Blue Feather had a big laugh. Jeremiah had speared an old moccasin.

Jeremiah had made a new friend. Blue Feather had taught him a new way to fish. By late afternoon he had speared four more fish.

"You must come to my camp one day," said Blue Feather, "and I will show you how to shoot a bow and arrow."

"Is that what that is?" said Jeremiah pointing to the bow and arrow strapped to Blue Feather's pony.

"Yes, we grow up learning to use the bow," said Blue Feather.

Jeremiah looked at the sky. He'd been away all morning, it was time to go home. "You must come to my house for supper. Do you know where I live?" asked Jeremiah.

"You live near the ridge of pines. I go the same way, then go that way to my village," said Blue Feather pointing east.

Jeremiah climbed onto his buckboard wagon and prepared to leave. "If you've forgotten, my name is Jeremiah."

Jeremiah was happy to have company for even a short distance. He liked his new friend. He wanted to know just how to use a bow and arrow and do some more spearfishing. He couldn't wait to tell his mother about his day.

As they traveled, the sky turned from friendly blue to dismal gray. Then the rumblings started. Jeremiah's horse began to whinny and pick up the pace. "Easy, June Bug, easy," said Jeremiah controlling the reins.

The rumblings got louder. Then it happened: a clap of thunder exploded. For a moment, not even the sound of the squeaky wagon or of the horse's hoofbeats were heard. Lightning lit up the sky like a Fourth of July celebration.

"The sky god is angry!" shouted Blue Feather, calming his horse.

Jeremiah snapped the reins for June Bug to go faster. Blue Feather gave his horse more freedom as they raced across the plains. A familiar noise began to echo in Blue Feather's ears as the ground underneath them began to shake. He brought his horse to a sudden stop.

"Whoa! Whoa!" screamed Jeremiah, pulling on the reins. "What's wrong?" he asked, watching Blue Feather.

Blue Feather jumped off his horse and put his ear to the ground.

"Stampede, buffalo stampede!" shouted Blue Feather.

Jeremiah turned around. What he saw looked like a swarm of bees in the distance but sounded like boulders falling down the side of a mountain.

"Jump on!" shouted Blue Feather, patting the back of his horse. Jeremiah was unsure if he should leave the only wagon and good horse he and his mother owned. But there was no chance

they could outrun the stampeding buffalo. He climbed on the back of Blue Feather's horse and the two raced ahead of the buffalo, who were coming closer.

Blue Feather's pony galloped with all the strength in his body. Jeremiah turned around, he didn't see June Bug or the wagon, just a wild herd of buffalo that were getting closer and closer.

Racing to outrun the buffalo, Blue Feather noticed something very strange ahead of him, the earth had separated. There was a wide gap his pony would have to jump. Slapping his pony's side with all his might, Blue Feather galloped faster and faster toward the opening in the ground.

"Aheeee!" yelled Blue Feather, as they leaped across. The hind hoof of the pony clipped the edge of the other side, but the pony quickly recovered and they made it. The raging buffalo kept running, some falling over the edge, the others turning away just in time. Jeremiah and Blue Feather rode back to the crevice and looked down. They saw a few dead buffalo piled on top of one another.

"I will tell my people about this place. They will come and take the skins and meat. We will have a great feast and heavy coats for the winter." Blue Feather smiled.

"We could have been killed," said a weary Jeremiah.

"But, we are alive. We must thank the sky god for this gift," said Blue Feather. He started dancing and chanting in the custom of his Cheyenne elders. All Jeremiah could do was watch and patiently wait for him to finish.

❖   ❖   ❖

It was late in the afternoon when Jeremiah arrived home. Both boys had experienced something that would keep them together for a long time.

"You can take your pony over to the barn, then come on in and have supper with us," said Jeremiah. He knew he had some explaining to do. After all, he had left with the only wagon his family owned and now he was back, without a wagon and without June Bug.

"Here chickee, chickee . . . come and get it," called Shelly. She was in the backyard feeding the chickens, Jeremiah heard her and ran around to the back of the house.

"Jeremiah Johnson, just where have you been all day?" she scolded.

"Mama, we got company for supper. Can he stay?" asked a cautious Jeremiah. By that time,

Blue Feather was standing next to him.

"Jeremiah, who is he?" she asked sternly.

"My friend, Blue Feather," said a proud Jeremiah.

Shelly stopped feeding the chickens and gave her son one of those looks that he knew so well. He'd have a lot of explaining to do later. "Blue Feather, welcome to our home. Jeremiah, you better set another place at the table."

Blue Feather had never tasted chicken cooked the way Jeremiah's mother cooked it. Her corn bread, squash, and black-eyed peas put a big smile on his face. He was unfamiliar with the use of a knife and fork, and he watched how Jeremiah used them, but he ate the chicken with his bare hands.

"I didn't hear the wagon when you came home and I didn't see it in the barn, Jeremiah," his mother said in a questioning tone, as she continued to eat.

"Mama, I hope you won't get angry, but there's no more wagon or June Bug. They were run over by a wild bunch of buffaloes," said Jeremiah. He told his mother all that had happened during the day and how Blue Feather saved his life. When he had finished his story, Shelly got up and hugged both of them.

"Thank you for saving my boy. You will

always be welcome in our home," she said tearfully.

"Can you stay the night?" asked Jeremiah.

"It's mighty late, you're welcome to stay," said Jeremiah's mother.

Before Blue Feather could say anything, Jeremiah had gone and pulled out some bedding. "You can sleep here on the floor next to me," said an excited Jeremiah.

"Won't your folks be worried about you?" asked Jeremiah's mother.

"If two moons have passed and I am not home, my people will come and find me," said Blue Feather.

Blue Feather spent the night, and early the next morning, he was up with the sun. He thanked Jeremiah and his mother, jumped on his pony, and galloped back to his camp.

Jeremiah had many chores to do that day. Storing the hay and plowing the fields was more difficult now that the wagon was gone. Without June Bug to pull the wagon, carrying a lot of things was fast becoming a major chore.

"Don't forget the roof, that sod is loose!" yelled his mother from across the fields.

Once he had filled the hayloft with hay, Jeremiah got the ladder. Carefully carrying the sod in a burlap sack, Jeremiah climbed onto the roof. While he was filling in the bare spots with fresh sod, his attention was drawn to the sound of hoofbeats. Coming in his direction, was a band of Cheyenne with horses pulling an empty wagon and the lead horse was June Bug. As they rode up to the house, Jeremiah's mother stopped what she was doing and started walking toward them. As she got closer, she recognized June Bug and her heart was happy again. Jeremiah came down from the roof.

"I am Running Fox. We come in peace. You are the friend of Blue Feather?" he asked.

"Yes, Blue Feather is my friend. What happened to him?" asked Jeremiah

"You and Blue Feather have given our people many buffalo hides and meat for the winter, He said that you lost the wagon and a good horse. We found the wagon and the horse you lost. We thank you," said Running Fox.

A smile slipped across Shelly's face, as big as the plains of Nebraska, as she patted June Bug on the chin.

"Bless you, Running Fox," Jeremiah's mother smiled, shaking his hand. Jeremiah was pleased with what his new friend had done, now his chores would be much easier.

Running Fox and his men departed in a cloud of dust and a whoop and holler. That night at dinner, Jeremiah's mother gave thanks for their blessings and prayed a special prayer for the safe return of her husband from the Civil War.

« 6 »

A Surprise Visitor

As the sun began to set on the Nebraska plains, Jeremiah was seated by the fire reading one of the books Mr. Stevenson had given him some time ago. His mother was writing in the diary she'd been keeping ever since they set foot in this part of the country.

"Have you heard from Papa yet?" asked Jeremiah.

"No . . . not in some time," his mother answered in a solemn voice.

"Do you think he's all right?" asked Jeremiah.

"It'd take a whole lot of them rebels to stop your papa, he'll be all right," she said.

Jeremiah was becoming bored with the book he was reading and picked up *The Three Musketeers*. The language was more difficult, but he liked the names of the heroes.

"Mama, do you remember where France is?" Jeremiah asked.

"Hmm, what, son?" she asked, her thoughts on other things.

"France, where is France?" repeated Jeremiah, carrying the book over to the table where she was writing. "See, right here." Jeremiah pointed to the word.

She recalled her reading lessons with Mrs. Stevenson long ago. "France is another country, far away from here," she said.

"Do you think they have slaves there?" Jeremiah wondered out loud.

"They might. Seems like wherever the white man is, he's trying to make slaves of somebody," his mother replied.

"Will people like us always be slaves, Mama?" asked Jeremiah.

"That's why your papa and other black men are fighting. They want to cut the neck off slavery like you do a poisonous snake. There are some good white folks who know slavery is bad for everybody. God doesn't make slaves, Jeremiah, people do," she said.

Their conversation was interrupted by the sound of a loud painful whinny. On his way to the door, Jeremiah heard it again. When he opened it, standing there, a few feet from the corral gate, was a beautiful young horse, bleeding from wounds all over his body.

"You came back . . . you came back!" shouted Jeremiah, running to the corral, his heart pounding like the wheels on a locomotive. It had been a year since Jeremiah had last seen the colt, and now he'd grown into a beautiful young stallion. When Jeremiah came near him, he saw deep cuts all over his body.

"What happened?" he asked as he carefully approached the scared animal. Judging by the slashes and rips of flesh, he had been attacked by a wild bear or a pack of coyotes. Blood was on his chest and back hooves.

"Looks like whatever got to you, you put up a good fight," said Jeremiah.

"Jeremiah, what is it?" shouted his mother from the front door.

"He's back, Mama, he's back!" shouted Jeremiah.

Jeremiah's mother hurried toward them. As she got closer, she could see the cuts. "Look at him, he's all cut up!"

"Some wild animal got to him, but he put up a fight. Look at his hooves," bragged Jeremiah.

"I know just what to put on those cuts. Take him into the barn and I'll get the ointment," she said.

Jeremiah took the young stallion by the mane and led him into the barn. This time he didn't pull away, but limped right along.

Whatever Jeremiah's mother put on those cuts seemed to work. The young horse was moving about like new after a few days. Jeremiah sat on the corral fence and watched the horse prance around the yard like he owned it.

"Did you ever name him?" asked his mother.

"No, I decided I wouldn't name him until I could ride him," said Jeremiah.

"Well, I guess he'll be on his way now, he looks good as new," said his mother.

Jeremiah decided to test the horse's memory, so he whistled. The young horse stopped running and slowly trotted over to him. Taller than he was over a year ago, Jeremiah didn't have to use the corral fence to mount his horse. He jumped down, met him in the middle of the corral, petted his neck, gripped his mane, and in one smooth motion, he was on the horse's back. Without the slightest whinny, the horse pranced around the corral. He had returned, no questions asked, and he had decided to stay.

"Looks like you finally got your pony," Jeremiah's mother smiled.

"He's no pony now, he's a stallion." beamed Jeremiah. The gate was open, so Jeremiah galloped straight through it. He was getting to know his new horse, and the stallion seemed to welcome his new rider. Jeremiah's mother wished Henry could see their son now, trotting around the yard so proud and confident.

"Be careful, he's still wild!" she yelled out.

Jeremiah was so taken by his new experience he didn't hear anything. He trotted his horse back over to the corral and dismounted.

"So, what are you going to name him?" Jeremiah's mother asked.

"I'm thinking," said Jeremiah, looking at his horse.

"I'll call him Cheyenne." said Jeremiah.

"Cheyenne?" she questioned.

"Blue Feather is my new friend, he's a Cheyenne, and my old friend came back to me," said Jeremiah, petting his horse's head.

"Somehow, I think your horse's name has something to do with friendship." his mother smiled.

The following morning Jeremiah planned to ride out to Blue Feather's camp. He wanted to show Blue Feather that his pony had returned as a beautiful chestnut-brown stallion. Jeremiah remembered Blue Feather telling him that his campgrounds were near a small creek where the pine trees lifted to the sky. When he rode up to the campgrounds he was greeted by a Cheyenne girl about his age. The young girl stared at him with a look of curiosity. "I am a friend of Blue Feather's. Where is he?" asked Jeremiah.

The girl glanced at Jeremiah and smiled. "You cannot go where he is, only the warriors go where Blue Feather is today. My name is Snowbird, I am Blue Feather's sister," she replied.

By now Jeremiah felt a little disappointed. He really wanted to see his friend. "When will Blue Feather be back?" asked Jeremiah.

"Soon." she said.

Taking the reins, he and Cheyenne walked with Snowbird past many different-shaped tepees where women were weaving baskets and mending clothes. They reached the far end of the camp. Jeremiah, leaving his horse outside, entered one of the biggest tepees in the camp. Sitting in the corner, painting a large clay pot, was a woman about Jeremiah's mother's age. She didn't pay them much attention until Snowbird broke her concentration.

"Mother, this is the friend Blue Feather spoke of. His name is Jeremiah."

"I am Morning Dove, mother of Blue Feather. He speaks well of you. He is with the warrior council. They will be back soon. Sit down and rest. Bring fresh water," she said to Snowbird.

"My son told me about the buffalo. You helped make many hides and meat for us," she continued.

"I owe my life to Blue Feather, his horse outran the buffalo. Thank you for returning the wagon and for the horses too," said Jeremiah.

Snowbird returned with a cup of cool water and handed it to Jeremiah. The sound of hoofbeats interrupted their conversation. The young braves had returned.

Snowbird ran out of the tepee to greet her brother. When Jeremiah walked out, wiping his mouth, he saw Blue Feather and other young Cheyenne braves with paint on their faces, arms, and legs.

"Jeremiah, my friend!" shouted Blue Feather.

"Blue Feather, is that you?" Jeremiah asked curiously. They hugged each other.

"Come with me," said Blue Feather, walking to the creek. He washed off the war paint.

"He came back to me, my pony," said a proud Jeremiah.

"Your horse, the one you set free?" questioned Blue Feather.

"That's him over there," pointed Jeremiah.

"He is a warrior stallion. What is the horse's name?" asked Blue Feather.

"Cheyenne, that's his name."

"Good name. Can he run?" Blue Feather smiled.

"Like the wind," replied Jeremiah.

"We will see," said Blue Feather. He pointed to the last tepee in his campsite. "We ride to there and back here. First horse to cross this spot is the fastest horse," challenged Blue Feather.

It was important for Blue Feather to win this race. All the other braves his age were cheering for him. The women weaving baskets stopped to watch one of their own ride the fastest stallion in the camp. Blue Feather's father, Chief Running Fox, stood proudly by his tepee as Blue Feather challenged his friend to a horse race.

Jeremiah and Blue Feather mounted their horses. They waited for the signal. Then a brave waved his hand and both boys slapped their horses.

Jeremiah had never raced before, but his horse, Cheyenne, had been running away from danger and into adventure for some time. He sensed Jeremiah needed him. "Come on, Cheyenne. Come on, boy, run!" whispered Jeremiah in his stallion's ear.

Cheyenne kicked into another speed, amazing everybody that watched the race. He shot past Blue Feather's horse like a speeding bullet. All Blue Feather could do was wipe the dust from his eyes.

After the race Blue Feather caught up with Jeremiah.

"Your stallion is the fastest horse I have ever seen. It is an honor to lose to such a warrior stallion like Cheyenne," said Blue Feather breathing heavily.

"He's something special all right. We're still friends?" asked a cautious Jeremiah.

"We will always be friends. You won this race, but when I teach you to shoot the bow and arrow, we'll see who's good at that." Blue Feather smiled .

Jeremiah and Blue Feather shook hands and agreed the next time they met, Blue Feather would teach Jeremiah how to use the bow and arrow. Jeremiah knew he had to get home, his mother would be very upset with him if he didn't complete his chores before dinner. Jeremiah waved good-bye to Blue Feather and galloped away.

❖   ❖   ❖

Dinner was especially good that evening. Jeremiah's mother moved with a little bounce in her step. She didn't say anything, but he could tell she was hiding something from him. He had an idea what it was.

"May I have another piece of blueberry pie?" asked Jeremiah.

"Sure you can, have as much as you want," his mother grinned. Jeremiah got up and walked over to the stove and heaped all that was left of the pie onto his plate.

When he came back to the table, his mother noticed his plate. Jeremiah just sat down casually and started to eat, glancing up, waiting for his mama to say something, "And when you finish that, there's another pie in the cupboard." She laughed.

"You heard from papa, didn't you?" Jeremiah smiled.

"Yes, I did, and he's alive! He said he got shot in the leg but the doctor patched him up and he's all right."

"Can I read the letter?" asked Jeremiah.

"Sure you can, just as soon as you finish all that pie," his mother said.

As he read his papa's letter, Jeremiah felt closer to him that ever before. Jeremiah was much taller now, and the pony his papa helped him catch over a year ago had grown into a beautiful chestnut brown stallion.

Life on the Nebraska plains was changing fast, thought Jeremiah, nothing was the same anymore. He wondered if his papa would be different when he came home. There was so much he wanted to tell him about Cheyenne, Blue Feather, and shooting a bow and arrow. Jeremiah continued to read his papa's letter, over and over into the night.